HECTOR

Based on *The Railway Series* by

Illustrations by
Robin Davies

EGMONT

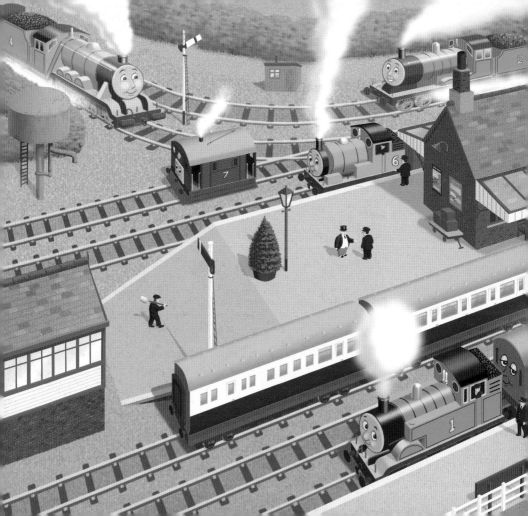

EGMONT

We bring stories to life

First published in Great Britain 2008
by Egmont UK Limited
239 Kensington High Street, London W8 6SA

Thomas the Tank Engine & Friends™

CREATED BY BRITT ALLCROFT

Based on the Railway Series by the Reverend W Awdry
© 2008 Gullane (Thomas) LLC. A HIT Entertainment company.
Thomas the Tank Engine & Friends and Thomas & Friends are trademarks of Gullane (Thomas) Limited.
Thomas the Tank Engine & Friends and Design is Reg. U.S. Pat. & Tm. Off.

HIT entertainment

ISBN 978 1 4052 3783 3
1 3 5 7 9 10 8 6 4 2
Printed in Italy

The Forest Stewardship Council (FSC) is an international, non-governmental organisation
dedicated to promoting responsible management of the world's forests. FSC operates a
system of forest certification and product labelling that allows consumers to identify
wood and wood-based products from well-managed forests.

For more information about Egmont's paper-buying policy please visit www.egmont.co.uk/ethicalpublishing

For more information about the FSC please visit their website at www.fsc.org

*T*his is the story of Hector the Horrid, a big black truck who told the engines to keep away. But when Thomas decided to teach him a lesson, he discovered that Hector was not as horrid as he looked …

Thomas the Tank Engine loves shunting Troublesome Trucks.

He can biff them harder and faster than any other engine.

It's one of his favourite jobs.

One morning, The Fat Controller had an important announcement.

"James and Edward must take extra deliveries of coal," he boomed.

"Thomas, you must shunt and fill trucks at the Coaling Plant for James and Edward to collect this afternoon," he added.

Thomas was very pleased.

Just then, Bill and Ben chuffed by with a big, black truck. It was biffing and bashing them.

"*Two* engines pushing *one* truck?" said Thomas.

"This is Hector," huffed Bill. "He hates being shunted. We call him Hector the Horrid!"

Bill and Ben chuffed slowly away with Hector.

"I could biff Hector firmly into place," Thomas boasted to James.

Later, Thomas chuffed into the Coaling Plant. And there was Hector.

The other trucks giggled. *"Big, bad and solid, he's Hector the Horrid*!" they sang.

Thomas puffed closer.

"KEEP AWAY!" roared Hector.

"Bill and Ben were right," thought Thomas, "Hector *is* horrid!"

Thomas decided to keep away. He spent the morning shunting the other trucks and filling them with coal.

All the time, Thomas could feel Hector the Horrid watching him.

The Plant Manager came to see Thomas. "We need an extra large delivery," he said. "You must shunt and fill Hector. Rosie is coming to help."

Later, Rosie puffed into the yard. She saw Hector. "Do we have to shunt that big truck, Thomas?" she peeped.

"Yes," puffed Thomas. "But he doesn't want to be shunted! His name is . . ."

Before Thomas could finish, Hector opened his mouth and let out the biggest roar ever!

"KEEP AWAY!" he bellowed.

Rosie was so surprised that she shook from funnel to footplate, and steamed straight out of the yard!

This made Thomas cross.

Hector had biffed and bashed Bill and Ben . . . He had shouted at Thomas . . . And frightened Rosie so much, that she had puffed away.

Now the extra delivery would never be ready!

Thomas had had enough! He puffed up to Hector . . . and biffed him!

Hector was cross. "KEEP AWAY!" he roared.

"I won't!" huffed Thomas. "You are causing confusion and delay! You really are horrid!"

Then with one mighty biff, Thomas pushed Hector backwards into a set of buffers. Hector couldn't stop, and rolled right off the track!

Thomas felt very bad. He hadn't meant to biff Hector so hard! He puffed over to the truck.

Hector lay on his side, looking very sad. Now Hector didn't seem so horrid.

"I'm sorry I biffed you so hard," wheeshed Thomas. "But why won't you be shunted?"

"I'm scared!" moaned Hector.

Thomas was surprised.

"I'm a new truck," Hector groaned. "I'm scared of being filled with coal. I've never done it before. That's why I didn't want to be shunted."

Thomas wanted to help Hector. "Sometimes I'm scared when I have to do something new," Thomas chuffed, "but coal isn't scary!"

Later, Rocky arrived. He lifted Hector back on to the tracks.

Hector watched Thomas roll under the hopper. Black, dusty coal poured into Thomas' coal box.

"See, it's not scary," Thomas peeped, kindly.

Then Hector smiled. "I'd like to be filled with coal, too," he rumbled.

So Thomas pulled Hector quickly under the hopper to fill him up with coal.

Thomas shunted Hector into place, just as James and Edward puffed into the yard.

They were surprised to see Hector there.

Soon, the trains were ready, and James and Edward puffed away to make their deliveries.

"Good luck!" Thomas whistled.

But the whistle wasn't for them. Thomas was tooting to his new friend, Hector, who wasn't horrid, after all!

The Thomas Story Library is THE definitive collection of stories about Thomas and ALL his friends.

5 more Thomas Story Library titles will be chuffing into your local bookshop in 2009!

Stanley
Flora
Colin
Hank
Madge

And there are even more Thomas Story Library books to follow late

So go on, add to your Thomas Story Library NOW!

A Fantastic Offer for Thomas the Tank Engine Fans!

STICK POUND COIN HERE

In every Thomas Story Library book like this one, you will find a special token. Collect 6 Thomas tokens and we will send you a brilliant Thomas poster, and a double-sided bedroom door hanger! Simply tape a £1 coin in the space above, and fill out the form overleaf.

TO BE COMPLETED BY AN ADULT

To apply for this great offer, ask an adult to complete the coupon below and send it with a pound coin and 6 tokens, to:
THOMAS OFFERS, PO BOX 715, HORSHAM RH12 5WG

☐ Please send a Thomas poster and door hanger. I enclose 6 tokens plus a £1 coin. (Price includes P&P)

Fan's name..

Address..

....Postcode...........................

Date of birth..

Name of parent/guardian...

Signature of parent/guardian...

Please allow 28 days for delivery. Offer is only available while stocks last. We reserve the right to change the terms of this offer at any time and we offer a 14 day money back guarantee. This does not affect your statutory rights.

☐ Data Protection Act: If you do not wish to receive other similar offers from us or companies we recommend, please tick this box. Offers apply to UK only.